DROPPING *your*
ROCK

DROPPING *your*
ROCK

Choosing Love over Judgment

❦

Nicole Johnson

W Publishing Group™

www.wpublishinggroup.com
A Division of Thomas Nelson, Inc.
www.ThomasNelson.com

Published by W Publishing Group, a Division of Thomas Nelson, Inc., P.O. Box 141000, Nashville Tennessee 37214.

ISBN 0-8499-1779-4

Printed in the United States of America
03 04 05 06 07 PHX 7 6 5 4 3 2

For Women of Faith
and Barbara Johnson

❧

Almost since the beginning of time, human beings have had a brutally simple way of dealing with wrong: rocks. Someone would point out the offender in the camp or the family or the clan, and everyone would come running. Picking up a cold, hard ballot of stone, they would violently cast their vote against wrong, again and again and again, until it was gone. It was their way.

But one hot day in the Middle East a man stepped in front of the rock throwers and changed things forever. A woman had been caught in the act. Not hearsay, not suspicion, not circumstantial evidence. Caught in the very act of adultery. Dragging her out, the men forced her to stand in front of the crowd as they pressed in on her angrily with rocks in their hands.

Clothes—if she had any on when they caught

her—had been torn off. Hot tears spilled down her cheeks in shame or maybe anger. Where was the man? Was she his heart's love or just the afternoon's activity? There is no way to know. Either way, he wasn't there; she was alone, and they were on her. They— the self-proclaimed upholders of moral righteousness, the superpious pillars of the community armed with their bludgeoning hypocrisy and crowd-pleasing indignation over wrong. Her stomach was knotted so tightly she could scarcely breathe. Her dignity was shredded, her spirit drenched with dread, but her hands were clenched in defiance. She'd sinned and been caught, and now she was dead-ended in a circle of judges with rocks in their hands.

Have you ever noticed how good it feels to throw a rock really hard? Your hand feels the weight of the

stone, and when you let it fly, there's a tremendous release. Is that what they felt that day? That each person's rock carried the weight of the community's judgment? It had become a familiar scene. "No," they would yell as they threw. "Wrong! Caught! Punish!" They would throw and throw, their fury fueled by each other as much as by the crime until the one in the center was still. And then they would revel in the grim release of sin avenged.

Problem is, rocks don't hit sin. Rocks hit people.

And thousands of years later, they still do.

Oh, we're too sophisticated nowadays to be flinging granite, but the words we throw in judgment and outrage are as hard and cold as any stone of old. And the release we feel when we let them go can be just as exhilarating.

Four teenagers get killed on a Friday night, and we hurl our rocks: "Well, they shouldn't have been drinking." No, they shouldn't have, but does that ease the guilt and the pain for their parents?

A young woman gets raped leaving a party, and someone says, "She was wearing a short skirt, and she deserves exactly what she got." We drag her into the circle and throw our rocks.

A businessman goes to jail for a poor decision involving other people's money, and we growl, "He can rot in there as far as I'm concerned." Never mind his wife and kids, we pile the rocks as high as we can.

A woman confronts someone rudely about an indiscretion in her life and later phones a friend to report, "And then I told her exactly what I thought of that sin." Whap! Now that woman will be in no

danger of appearing soft on wrong—while the woman she hit will wear the bruise.

As we throw, we convince ourselves that if the rock lands in just the right spot, it can knock out something evil. You remember the story of David and Goliath. Plant the rock squarely in the forehead of your foe, and your side wins. If our goal is to kill our enemy, this could be the answer. But if we hope to change a friend's heart, it definitely is not. We can sometimes knock sense into a person with a rock, but we can't knock out sin.

Remember the scene in the movie *Forrest Gump* where Jenny goes back to her childhood house after years of being gone? She stares at the old shack where her daddy—her trusted daddy—would come to her bed at night and use her like a trash receptacle.

She picks up a little rock and flings it at the house, breaking a window. She stares and stares as tears start to sting, and then she hurls another rock as hard as she can. She throws and throws, another and another, flinging and crying until she collapses on the ground. Quietly and in his simple way, Forrest pronounces, "Sometimes there just aren't enough rocks."

And there aren't. Jenny was hurling those rocks at something bigger. She threw with all her might, venting years of pain, at what that house represented: sin, the blackness that overcomes hearts and makes people unrecognizable as human beings. *But there aren't enough rocks in the entire world to beat out sin.*

If we actually could throw a rock and hit the evil in the world, we would still run out of rocks before it was all gone. For all the wrongs that have been done

to us, there simply are not enough rocks in the world to make it all right. Would there ever be enough rocks for the Holocaust survivors? Would every quarry in the state of Oklahoma yield enough stones for a man who would blow up a building, killing 168 people whose only crime was showing up for work? All the rock throwing in the universe cannot calm what aches and burns in our souls when we have been horribly wronged. We cannot set the bone of what is broken on the earth with a cast of jagged rocks.

When that one man stepped out of the crowd of rock throwers that day and scribbled in the sand, he reminded a group of angry people who wanted to beat the sin out of her that it just wasn't possible. And he wasn't going to let them try just so they could feel better. They could kill her, but it wouldn't solve the

bigger problem. And he had come to solve the bigger problem so we wouldn't have to try with our little, pathetic rocks.

What did Jesus scribble in the sand that day? The names of men in the crowd who had also slept with her? That would have gotten their attention. Did he just trace patterns in the sand to allow tempers time to cool? Even group vengeance can be stopped if the momentum slows. Or did he write something completely different, such as "She is your daughter"? That would have changed how they felt. Whatever he wrote, he drove it home with these words: "If any one of you is without sin, let him be the first to throw a stone at her."

Silence.

No one could say anything. His words disarmed all their accusations. He cut away the false high ground

from under the feet of the self-righteous and for all time leveled the playing field between accused and accusers. He gave those of us who have made the worst choices of our lives a place where it is safe to be broken without fear of being destroyed. He showed us that no matter what, he would stand between us and our judges.

And whenever we find ourselves part of the angry circle of the rock throwers with our own rock raised, he confronts us with the freedom to choose love over judgment. He didn't make the accusers drop their rocks. He never does. He just challenged them to consider their own hearts, saying, in essence, "Deal with yourself before you deal with anyone else." Because he knows how prone we are to judge others.

The two things we judge most harshly are those things we don't struggle with at all and those things

we struggle with the most. If we don't struggle with an issue, it's easy to take a hard line and have no compassion. It isn't our problem, so we don't understand why it's anyone's problem. If we do struggle with an issue, we may be the harshest judge of all, because we condemn most vehemently in others the very things we try to deny in ourselves. Our own hearts are deceitful, and Jesus said be very, very careful before we judge, because if we judge others by the rock, others will judge us by the rock. But judge with love, and we'll be judged with love.

Most of us are used to lining up on the loveless side of judgment; we've been doing it for years. We've grown up in the rock rodeo, becoming champion throwers at our favorite sins. We can hit what we think is the bull's-eye from a hundred yards or more.

But then the day dawns that we come running with our rock, and our hand freezes at the realization that we are throwing at our own sin, and we'll hit ourselves in the process. Or we arrive at the circle just in time to see the one forced into the center is our loved one. Or maybe one day our door is thrown open, and to our horror the circle of hate and rocks is closing in on us.

These are drop-your-rock moments.

Love is giving us a chance to choose.

Such moments come at different times for each of us, as when that sin we found so easy to hate now has a face and eyes, maybe even our own. And what was so simple for us to judge before, now convicts us deeply or breaks our hearts.

When this happens—when your son tells you

he's homosexual, your best friend confesses in agony she's having an affair, or your sister tearfully describes her abortion—you have a choice to leave mere theory behind and enter the gritty reality of relationship. As you listen, your teeth clench, and anger erupts, and your grip on the rock tightens. You want to throw it so badly. You want to say exactly what you think of that sin and try to beat it out of them. You've done it a hundred times before, hitting the anonymous "sinner," but now it's painfully different.

Love is giving you a chance to choose.

Seeing our own loved one in the circle is the most poignant challenge of all, for it invites us for the first time to step between the accusers and our beloved. And we can see in the mirror of our own emotions the way we've shut people out by the rigid compartments

and categories we've created. We can see how callously and carelessly we've treated others because their wrong never significantly touched our lives. We can see this, because it never hurt before. Not like this. And we stare at the ugly face of judgment in the mirror.

We drop our rocks, and they fall to the ground with a flat thud of grace.

If the adulterous woman had been someone's beloved, the people might have dropped their rocks for her. But she wasn't. She was an easy target for them to hit because she meant nothing to them and she was blatantly wrong. Which made it easy for the people to hide behind her sin. There was no one in the crowd without blackness in his heart, but would any one of them acknowledge that? If they could scorn her sin publicly, they would not have to think about their own.

So there she stood, possibly naked, a little defiant, but mostly ashamed.

She fell to her knees and closed her arms tightly around herself as she braced for the first rock. She waited in agony, afraid to hope as she stared at the dirt becoming mud with her tears. She couldn't stop replaying the images of that morning. Door thrown open. Being forced outside and dragged through the streets. They would never let her go. She was so clearly caught.

Lost in her own thoughts, she almost missed the soft little thump of a rock falling to the ground, then another and another. Then shuffling. Then stillness.

His voice alone broke the silence. "Woman, where are your accusers?"

Eyes downcast, she saw no feet around her,

just rocks lying here and there. Still she could not lift her head.

Everyone else was gone. Only he was left.

In a tender voice he asked, "Has no one condemned you?"

"No man, Lord," she said, perhaps meaning, "You are a man but more than a man. What will you do to me?" She was now at the mercy of God, and he was about to speak. He could have said, "Now that they've all gone, I want to tell you what I think of your behavior." But he didn't. For the record, he said, "Neither do I condemn you."

For the first time since the ordeal began, she lifted her head.

When we have done wrong, there is no sweeter moment in all of life than to feel the forgiveness

of God. His words told her that it was all right, despite all that was wrong.

And then he said one more thing: "Go and sin no more."

The same Love that called the others to drop their rocks was also giving her a chance to choose. Continue the sickening slavery of wrong, or walk in the freedom of forgiveness. There was a fork in the road for her, too.

Grace doesn't just let us off; it sets us free. With one blow it strikes the shackle, breaking it open so we may walk unfettered in freedom. It promises us a better tomorrow than the today we've made for ourselves. "Go and sin no more."

The "go" is the grace.

No matter what happened next, she would not be

punished for her crime that day. He'd granted her an undeserved pardon wrapped in magnificent forgiveness. She was free to go free.

The "sin no more" is the cost of staying free.

Could she really sin no more? It depends on which road she chose with her freedom. Would she go back to her old life, hunting furtively through the streets for the man she'd been with? Or would she feel the powerful strength that real love and forgiveness had just given her, hold her head high, and never look back? Go and sin no more.

Love appears to allow evil to run right over it. But isn't that part of love's glorious strategy? In the drama of this world, the play wasn't over after act 2. At the climax of the conflict when it looked like evil and judgment would win, the plot took a surprise

twist: the author stepped into the play. He revealed the hidden power of love, giving us a divine show and tell we would never forget. And that changed everything.

Our rocks will never change the world, only pockmark it with hate and fear. Throwing rocks will never make us more loving. As we clutch and throw our rocks, we reveal our pettiness and our inability to change our own lives. Only when we drop our rocks and choose to love do we become more loving.

So the next time someone trembles in fear and tells you something you really didn't want know, or you see your sin in someone else's life, or your loved one is braced to feel your stone cold words, you'll know what to do. Loosen your grip, and listen for the flat thud of grace as you choose love over judgment. The only one who has the right to throw a rock

is the one who has never done any wrong. Ever. The only one who is without blackness in his own heart. The one who has never taken anything from anyone else, never compromised his own standards, never lied even a little to make himself look better. There has been only one, and only that one can pick up the rock.

And he did. He became the Rock and took care of our wrong for all time. And he still stands between us and our accusers. And he still lifts our heads and sets us on the path of freedom. When he knelt in the sand that day, just maybe he wrote these words: "My rock is bigger than yours, and I will handle this one." *Rock of Ages, cleft for me, let me hide myself in Thee . . .*

Love is still giving us the chance to choose.

About the Author

✌

Nicole Johnson is an actress, writer and television producer. She is the author of *Fresh Brewed Life* and a dramatist with Women of Faith. She makes her home in Santa Monica.

The Faith, Hope, and Love Trilogy

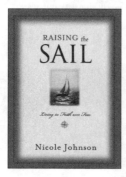

RAISING THE SAIL

Just as sailboats are made for the wind, women are made for relationships, and with both it takes faith to overcome the fear to let go and trust God's direction. Instead of frantically paddling or "motoring" our way through the seas of our emotional connections with each other, she challenges us to freely let go and trust the "Windmaker," God Himself, to help us find our way.

STEPPING INTO THE RING

Where is the woman, old or young, who will not shed a tear but silently scream in her heart as she walks in these pages through the diagnosis of breast cancer and the devastation that ensues? While she focuses on the specific soul-chilling crisis, Nicole offers her readers broader insights for dealing with major losses of all kinds. She extends genuine hope and much-needed rays of light to those who are mired in hopelessness and despair.

DROPPING YOUR ROCK

You can express your moral outrage by joining the angry mob howling for a sinner to be stoned. But what if that sinner is your friend, and you would rather change her heart than shed her blood? We don't have to hurl the rocks we clutch in our judgmental hands. With tender words and touching photos, Nicole Johnson guides us toward the "flat thud of grace" that can change our lives when we drop our rocks and choose to love instead.

Available May 2003 from Nicole Johnson

WOMEN OF FAITH

KEEPING A PRINCESS HEART

Every little girl grew up hearing the stories of "happily ever after," but finds it hard to believe that such a world still exists today. *Keeping a Princess Heart* is a deeply thoughtful exploration of the tension women feel between what they *long for* and what they *live with*. Women will discover how to hold on to their dreams as they take a deep, trusting dive into the wonderful world of fairy tales to reclaim a hidden treasure: a princess heart.

W PUBLISHING GROUP™
www.wpublishinggroup.com